938837

E
Wo

Wood, Audrey.
Weird parents   3.4

DATE DUE

NOV 17		MAR 28	MS
DEC 15		MAR 17	MS
FEB 4		MAR 10	GS
OCT 10		JAN 28	M.D.
OCT 26		MAY 09	E.P
DEC 19		JUN 01	
OCT 09		F D	
OCT 24			
NOV -4			
NOV -8			
JUN 05			
DEC 01			
FEB 10			
MAR 08			
NOV 29	G R		
DEC 11	R M		
A.S.	JAN 02		
MAY 21	BC		

GAYLORD   PRINTED IN U.S.A.

WEIRD PARENTS

AUDREY WOOD

Dial Books for Young Readers

NEW YORK

Published by Dial Books for Young Readers
A Division of Penguin Books USA Inc.
375 Hudson Street
New York, New York 10014

Published simultaneously in Canada
by Fitzhenry & Whiteside Limited, Toronto
Copyright © 1990 by Audrey Wood
Design by Nancy R. Leo
All rights reserved
Printed in Hong Kong
by South China Printing Co. (1988) Limited
First Edition
W
1 3 5 7 9 10 8 6 4 2

Library of Congress Cataloging in Publication Data
Wood, Audrey.
Weird parents / written and illustrated by Audrey Wood.
p.   cm.
Summary: A young boy comes to accept his parents' unusual
behavior, which includes packing surprises in his lunch box and
greeting strangers they meet on the street.
ISBN 0-8037-0648-0.
ISBN 0-8037-0649-9 (lib. bdg.)
[1. Parent and child—Fiction.] I. Title.
PZ7.W846We 1989   [E]—dc19   88-25742   CIP   AC

*The art for each picture was created using colored pencils,
watercolor wash, and pen and ink. It was then color-separated
and reproduced in full color.*

PARCHEESI is a registered trademark of
Milton Bradley Company.

For Arthur Levine,
who has weird parents too.

There once was a boy who had
weird parents.
No matter how many times he told them not to,
the weird parents did weird things whenever
they went out into the world.

In the morning the weird mother always walked the boy to his bus stop.

"Bye-bye, honeycakes!" she'd call.

Then as the bus drove away, she'd blow a huge kiss
and press her hand to her heart.

At twelve o'clock when the boy opened his lunchbox, he'd always have a weird surprise.

And in the afternoon the weird father always walked
him home. But not before he shook hands with
everyone he met.

"Pleased to meet you. How do you do? Isn't it a
lovely day?" he'd say.

More than anything, the boy dreaded the family's
night out on the town. Every Saturday evening

the weird father put on his weird hat and the weird
mother combed her hair in a weird way.

Then they would dance all the way down the stairs
to their weird car.

They were always early for the picture show, so the boy had to stand in line with them.

The weird mother always talked about the boy as if
he wasn't there.

"My son has a belly button that sticks out. No one
else in our family has one like it."

And the weird father always asked the boy to do
something silly.

"Walk like a chicken," he'd say.

Of course the boy wouldn't, so the weird father did
it instead.

When the movie began, the boy tried to enjoy it,

but his weird parents always laughed out loud when
no one else did.

At least things got better after the movie. The weird
father always treated them to ice cream cones. And the
weird mother always let the boy pick out a comic book.

At home they all played a double round of Parcheesi.®
And the weird parents never got mad if the boy won
both games.

And when they tucked him into bed and kissed him good night, the weird parents always sang a little song.

"Sweet dreams,
We love you,
Good night,
Now don't let the bedbugs bite,
Don't let the bedbugs bite."

But as the boy lay in bed trying to go to sleep, he couldn't

help wishing his parents weren't weird anymore.

Then he wished everyone else had weird parents.

Yet he knew that wasn't possible.

And somehow it didn't matter....

After all...

they were his parents, weird or not.